The Forever Team
Suzie Ivy

The Forever Team

Suzie Ivy

This is a work of fiction. ALL characters are derived from the author's imagination.

Dedicated to Sheriff Deputy Philip Anthony Rodriguez

End of Watch April 21, 2007

You will be forever in my heart.

Chapter One

Detectives work best in teams. It's that whole right brain, left brain scenario. In a good, well-established team what one person misses the other zeros in on. That's what I lost when my partner Tony died of cancer. It's been two years and I still can't find that someone who complements me, pushes me to be a better detective, and puts up with my moods. Not to mention my outside-the-box speculations of possible events in a crime. Tony was always first to congratulate me when I was dead-on, even after making fun of my leap from evidence to outrageous. He also pointed out when I was wrong and made sure I remembered several times over.

My department has five detectives and I'm odd man out, or in my case, woman out. Of thirty-two certified officers, I'm one of three females, and the only female detective. I work in a man's world. That's another reason Tony and I meshed. He didn't care that I was a woman. He wanted to solve cases, and the two of us were darned good at it.

Together.

For the past two years, I coasted along barely making the motions. I continued solving cases, but not at the same rate as Tony and I had managed to do. I also tried working with different detectives looking for that spark I had with Tony. Don't get me wrong, my relationship with Tony was in no way boyfriend/girlfriend. He was happily married to Beth, and Beth and I were close. We stayed in touch for a while after Tony died; a drink now and then with happy and sad memories of the man we both loved. Now, after two years, she was getting married again this fall. I knew because I had received a "save the date" card. Of all the stupid things to come up with in an already ridiculous event called weddings, they added save the date. A fork lodged in my throat was more appealing. And to make it worse, once Beth hit the dating market again, our friendship had dwindled. Her life without Tony moved on. Mine was ending here today at a dog kennel.

Yes, an overdramatic statement, but in my opinion accurate. After years of grievances made against me by fellow officers and detectives, my sergeant, Lou Spence, stopped listening to my excuses. He was partnering me with a dog. A trained K9—the miracle partner. One who never filed complaints.

Our first conversation on the subject was brief.

"How do you feel about dogs, Detective Jolett?" he asked as he leafed through a stack of papers.

"I've dated a few." I paused a moment thinking he'd look up, but he didn't, so I continued. "They smell and need a tight choke collar with a few kibbles thrown their way every now and then. It doesn't help much, though, and they generally remain an all-around nuisance." I was trying to push the sergeant's buttons, but it didn't seem to work. He didn't acknowledge my condescending reply in the slightest.

"Here, take this." He handed me a small packet. "Your training begins Monday at 0800. You'll be gone for eight weeks. Don't worry about your cases; they're being reassigned. Make arrangements with your current mongrel so he knows you'll be out of town." He looked directly into my eyes and the corners of his toward the back of the room. He or she refused to give me or Jack the time of day.

"Who's that?" I pointed at the reticent dog.

Jack looked between me and the Rottweiler a few times before answering. "That's Suii. He's lazy and getting up there in age. He has maybe two years left before he's retired."

I had eight, but we were sorta equal if you stretched it by comparing human years to dog years. "Bring him out." That was another thing about Jack; my short, clipped phrases apparently didn't irritate him. He opened the cage.

Suii lifted his head seemingly uncaring. Jack snapped his fingers. The dog slowly uncurled his massive body while gaining his feet. Big. Darn big. I'd judge Suii pushed one-fifty. The dog walked out of the cage and sat beside Jack's legs. It was a slouching sit. Lazy. The perfect dog for me.

Jack attached a leash and handed me the end. Suii didn't budge. Jack just looked at me, waiting to see what I'd do. I gave a firm tug and snapped my fingers. Just as slowly as Suii came out of his cage, he walked the three feet separating us and sat-slouched again. His huge head tipped sideways and back as his big chocolate eyes stared into mine.

I didn't take it as dominance. The dog appraised me like I appraised him. "I have a large couch, a television, and a small back patio. If you can handle that, I'll take you," I said in a no-nonsense tone.

His head cocked a little more and his floppy ears lifted just a bit. I took that as an affirmative and looked at Jack. "When do we go home?"

"We can start the next phase of training right now. Suii's trained in German. You'll have two additional weeks to become acquainted and learn his language before you can leave. Do you have questions about him, like why he's here?"

I really didn't care, but nodded anyway. Jack obviously had something to say.

He looked down at the dog and his lips compressed. "His handler left him in the car. The call went bad, and Officer Bradly was shot and killed. Suii hasn't bonded with anyone since, so don't get your hopes up. He's unenthusiastic and can be difficult."

Jack just described me and I was relieved—bonding was something I didn't need. Suii and I would get along just fine.

Chapter Two

Suii was lazy, stubborn, and perfect. He went through our last two weeks of training with his tongue hanging out while panting up a storm and dribbling saliva everywhere. Jack told me Rotts aren't good as service dogs in warmer climates because they don't acclimate well. Though my K9 training took place in the mid-spring heat of Tucson, I made my home in Northern Arizona. I was past ready to return to a cooler climate.

Suii performed his tasks with the least amount of effort required and didn't seem to care about too much except the heat. Whenever possible, he stretched his leash to any conceivable inch of shade he could find. He also plopped his large body down with a big huff if I wasn't paying attention. The dog did not understand parade rest. His interpretation was parade lounge—a large, floppy sprawl. I secretly cheered him on if Jack wasn't looking.

I think Jack felt Suii and I didn't match, but my mind was set. I finished the two weeks without complaining…much. After receiving Suii's documentation on graduation day, we headed to my car. I had a green, unmarked patrol unit with a K9 cage in the back. Suii jumped in with a quick wag of his stub tail and off we went. I turned the air conditioner to high and adjusted the radio to the latest pop music. Suii stretched out in the back and slept. We didn't need to stop for a pee break because Suii's bladder was as large as mine.

After entering Pierce city limits and heading down the block that led to my home, I turned the radio down and carried on a one-way conversation with the suddenly attentive dog in the back. "I have a neighbor you can terrorize. Treats are in it for you if you do a good job. He has a twerpy little rat for a dog otherwise known as a Shih Tzu. You can eat him if the neighbor isn't looking." I glanced into the rearview mirror and saw Suii's head lift higher and his ears cock. "I don't go back to work until Wednesday, so you and I can be lazy and catch up on TV shows."

A long whine sounded from the backseat as Suii returned his head to his favorite position of flopped down on any available object. If I understood his whine correctly, he liked the same shows I did or he liked the idea of being lazy. It was hard to tell.

Sure enough, as I pulled in front of my townhome, Mr. Knock-toes, as I called him because of his pigeon walk, came toward my vehicle with Craptzu, my nickname for the rat, snuggled in his arms. Whenever I came home, I found small piles of dog poo in the five-by-ten strip of grass I called a yard. Always on my grass and no other. Brown pee spots also peppered the small space. No one else in our vicinity had a small dog, and it didn't take a detective to solve this crime.

I opened my door and walked around to the back with the leash. This would be tricky. I opened Suii's door, clipped the leash onto his collar, and stepped back. With my right hand, I made a motion toward Mr. Knock-toes. "Fass," I whispered in German. For the first time, I saw all of Suii's powerful glory in action. He even managed to surprise me by pulling me forward several feet before I gained control. "Nein, nein," I shouted as Suii almost removed my arm at the shoulder.

He immediately stopped, but continued growling, completely overpowering the terrified yips coming from Craptzu and the unmanly screams coming from Mr. Knock-toes. I didn't stick around to see if my neighbor's pants matched my name for his dog. "Hier," I said. *Come*, in English. Suii followed me with loud, I'll-kill-you-and-your-little-dog-too, growls.

Priceless.

I entered my home and shut the door before laughter ruined our bad-dog routine. "Good dog, what a good dog," I told him while using the high-pitched play voice I'd learned during training.

With a huge grin, I walked Suii to the back door and opened it. "Not much, but it's your kingdom, so mark your territory while I bring in our things." I closed the back door as soon as Suii passed through and headed back out to my car. My neighbor was nowhere in sight, and for the first time since Tony's death, self-satisfaction settled over me. Such a small victory, but it made me happy.

During the next few days, Suii and I settled in. I worked with him for two hours each day and meticulously wrote in his training manual to show the training time we put in. The rest of the time we vegged. Suii wasn't fond of my kale chips and I wasn't fond of his dog biscuits, but we made it work. He stayed on his side of the room and I stayed on mine. At night he lay in front of my bedroom door. Best of all, I complained and he listened without adding his two cents.

Chapter Three

I awoke early on Wednesday for my first day back at work after eight weeks away. During the past two years I had used endless cups of coffee to get my bleary eyes and rear in gear. With only one cup and Suii at my side, I didn't need the extra boost today. Maybe I'd needed a vacation for a long time instead of drowning myself in work. Not that I hadn't worked hard in K9 training, but it was different. As much as it upset me to lose my active cases, the break did me good, and there was something to be said about working with a dog. I fully admit to a quick change in attitude about acquiring a K9 because the dog's aloof behavior was growing on me.

Suii jumped in the backseat after we both stopped and looked closely at the front grass.

No crap and no sign of Craptzu. A decent start to my day.

The ride to the department took less than ten minutes. I entered my pin code at the gate and waited for the large rolling fence to slide back. Though the temperature was in the low sixties, the sun was shining. I parked under the only tree in the lot which provided the only spot of shade. I would let Sergeant Spence know I was permanently claiming this parking space.

I planned to leave the car running with Suii inside the vehicle while I ran inside to see what case files were open and get myself back into the grind. I closed my car door and walked several feet from the car when Suii decided to find his voice. It was different than I'd heard from him so far—half bark, half whine and very loud. "Nein. Phui." *No. Shame.* I spoke sharply. I took another step and his dog wails grew louder. A few more steps and the barking whines turned to a full-out howl.

Crap. For a big tough mutt this was embarrassing.

I walked back to my door and opened it to grab the leash. Suii immediately ended his tantrum. I opened his door and attached his lead so he could jump out. "Who has who trained here, you big baby?" I muttered as I entered another code into the outside squad room door. I marched in, Suii at perfect heel, and nodded to the officers sitting and typing at their desks. The two who looked up nodded back, but no one said anything. I wasn't one who invited petty conversation at the best of times. With one-hundred and fifty pounds of muscled teeth beside me, things wouldn't be changing any time soon. I marched to my sergeant's office and walked in after a compulsory knock against the open door.

I used the most syrupy voice possible when I said, "Detective Jolett and K9 Suii reporting for duty, sir."

Sergeant Spence's head came up from his endless paperwork and he smiled. Lou was a nice guy, a demanding sergeant, and a great cop whom I appreciated whenever he wasn't on my crap-list.

"Glad to have you back and glad to meet our newest officer," he said while looking at the dog sitting by my leg.

"This is Suii. His disposition is equal to mine and so far we've hit it off. I'm hoping you have some work for me and I don't need to hustle up my own cases." It wasn't uncommon for detectives to cruise town when things were slow and keep an eye out for the deadbeats who made up the majority of our workload. If they weren't in trouble, they were planning it, and sometimes we got lucky when being observant.

"May I approach Suii?" Lou asked as he slowly stood from his desk.

"Bleib." *Stay*, I commanded Suii. "Approach at your own risk," I said with a smile.

"You know I was a handler for twenty years. It's good to see a K9 again. The department has needed one for a while."

We had a drug dog with its handler attached to the county drug task force. Suii was the first K9 attached to the department. Lou approached slowly. I handed him the leash. "He's trained in German."

"Heir." *Come*, Lou said without missing a beat.

It surprised me when Suii didn't immediately snap to the command. His mammoth head tilted my way and I received a *what the heck* look from big brown eyes.

"Pass auf!" *Pay attention*, I told Suii.

Lou repeated his command and Suii meandered to his side. Suii expelled a large huff of air and plopped his body down on the floor. No sit in sight. He wasn't happy with me. Lou bent down and ran his fingers through the dog's fur, ignoring Suii's lapse in manners.

"He's an embarrassment to the department," I muttered.

"He's a darn fine dog. I spoke to Jack Mallory and he said the two of you did well together."

I had no idea how Sergeant Spence kept a straight face with that statement. During my training, I was surly at best and Suii did the bare minimum to get by. "May I have my fur bucket back?" Before I could even hold out my hand for the leash, Suii was up and headed my way.

"The two of you are bonding." Lou said as he handed over the leash.

"Bonding my hind-end. I hand out the cookies and he knows it. About those cases?"

"On your desk. Call dispatch and give them Suii's badge number. I'll send over an official order in the next hour."

I walked to the door and looked over my shoulder before stepping out. "And what is Suii's badge number?"

"David Sixteen."

\* \* \*

I stared at the far wall of my office with Suii curled at my feet. D16, phonetically David Sixteen on the radio, meaning Detective Sixteen. That had been Tony's badge number. I was upset. My hand rested on the phone, but I couldn't bring myself to call dispatch. I felt a cold nudge to my other hand and noticed Suii standing beside my desk. His large tongue came out and slathered the same hand with slobber. Uck. "That's gross, you know?"

A low "Whii" came from his throat.

This was the first time he'd shown me affection. I think Suii could tell I was upset and that had my mood lightening slightly. I rubbed my hand over his head, traveling to the underside of his neck to give a few scratches. "You will never be half the partner as Tony, but I guess you can have his badge number." I picked up the phone and called dispatch.

D14 and D16 were a team again.

Chapter Four

Other than the ever-present pile of fur by my side each day, my first week back at work was uneventful. I heard a few snide comments about the new female at the department, but I didn't care enough to tell them Suii was a neutered male. The whispers were muttered far enough away that Suii's leash didn't reach. Unfortunately, it would be obvious if I let it go and gave the attack command. My fellow detectives gave Suii a bit more respect. None would argue about me being a darn good detective, but I'd never win Miss Congeniality either.

Tony was well-liked by his brothers in blue and opened doors for me. I'd played nice to please Tony. Small talk, gossip, and bull crap weren't my thing, but Tony said it's what made a police department a well-oiled machine. Blah, blah, and blah. Tony was no longer around to keep me in the loop. Suii and his large, powerful jaws actually took me further out of the loop. And the point goes to my K9. I liked it this way.

The first day of my second week with Suii changed my attitude toward my new sidekick. I was headed to a woman's house to interview her about her car being stolen the week before. We'd recovered the vehicle and discovered her son was the culprit. She'd withheld information about her son living with her and disappearing at the same time as the car. I was considering filing a felony complaint against her. There was nothing I hated more than wasted time and now that she didn't want to press charges, my hours spent on the case were worthless. I would make my decision after giving her a chance to explain her actions.

I was around the corner from her home when a domestic-in-progress call, which is a family fight, came over the radio. I was familiar with the couple living at this address. In a mid-sized department, detectives backed up patrol officers from time to time. This particular husband and wife had small children who suffered because of the home violence. Several times we tried having them removed from the home, but so far neither child had bruises or showed outward psychological problems because of their parents' behavior, so our efforts failed.

I pressed the button on my mic. "David Fourteen and Sixteen on scene, please send backup patrol." Usually, I would never enter a domestic situation before backup arrived, but Suii changed things. I parked two houses down and grabbed my outer ballistic vest, tugged it over my head, and fastened the heavy-duty Velcro strips so it fit snuggly. It held a Taser, cuffs, rubber gloves, and a flashlight. I attached Suii's leash and we headed to the front door. Suii growled at the same time I heard a woman scream. The children began screaming in the background too. I turned the knob on the front door and found it unlocked.

"Police," I said as I opened the door with my gun pointed down. Daryl, the husband, had his wife on the floor beating the tar out of her and didn't look up when I entered. The two kids were cowering at the edge of the hallway. Daryl lifted his arm and struck his wife in the face again. She'd stopped screaming at the first punch I witnessed, and I believed she was now unconscious.

"Back off," I yelled at Daryl while pointing my gun in his direction. Suii's growling continued but he obeyed my commands and didn't pull on the leash while my gun was drawn. Daryl didn't look at the gun though, he looked at Suii. The dog's low growls had Daryl's eyes opening wide. Then, stupid man that he was, he pulled his fist back again. "Fass," I said as I dropped Suii's lead.

One hundred and fifty pounds of muscle and teeth descended on Daryl. His scream was louder than the children's. Suii tore him away from Melody.

"Stop moving and he'll back off," I yelled several times over the screaming. Daryl finally froze.

"Officer Franks behind you," I heard over my shoulder.

"Call an ambulance," I said as I walked to check on Melody. She blinked rapidly, obviously disoriented. "You with me, Mel?" I asked.

"The kids," she said as she began crying.

"They're safe." I could still hear them crying. Melody slowly turned her head and saw Suii standing over her husband with Daryl's bloody arm enclosed in the dog's jaws.

"Call your dog off and I'll cuff him," Officer Franks said.

"Suii, aus." *Let go*.

With another growl, Suii released Daryl and came to my side. I grabbed his lead.

"We've got an ambulance on the way, Melody. Stay down so you don't make your injuries worse. I'll check on the kids."

I turned and approached the children. I wasn't thinking about the fear they must have for the big dog who just took down their father. Suii did, though. He slunk his huge body low and as close to the floor as he could get while crawling closer to the kids. Their large, terrified eyes never left the dog. I pulled back on Suii's lead, but he crawled another foot and rolled to his back whining.

The older girl put her hand out and ran it over Suii's belly. "He…he… hurt my mommm… mommy," she cried with a trembling voice.

At first I thought she meant Suii, but then realized she meant her father. Before I could stop her, she threw her arms around Suii and practically climbed on top of him. Suii licked her tear-stained face as gently as if she was his baby. The other child, a two- or three-year-old boy, tentatively placed his hand out and rubbed a patch of Suii's belly that wasn't covered by his sister.

I turned back to Officer Franks who had Daryl handcuffed and was holding him by the shoulder. I'm not sure whose face was more surprised, mine or the officer's. We had one in custody, two calmed children, and Melody following my orders by lying still.

The ambulance crew walked in. "We need to check the kids?" one of them asked.

Suii gave a low growl still lying on his back. I would swear the darned dog understood exactly what the E.M.S. attendant asked. I held out my hand so the attendant didn't come closer to the kids. "No, check mom first and then dad. Mom was unconscious for a short time and needs to be transported. Dad will need a few teeth punctures tended before he goes to jail."

"I'm suing the entire department for what that dog did to me." Daryl was back to being stupid, so I ignored him.

I focused on the children and lowered my voice. "Hey, guys, how about we step outside and give the ambulance crew a little more room. Suii will stay with you. He needs some more love from the two of you because he's scared."

The oldest looked up at me from her perch on top of Suii. "He's not scared. He's brave."

He sure the heck was. I helped the little girl stand and handed her Suii's lead. "Can you walk him outside and I'll carry your brother?" She took the leash and the three of us went outside. When we were at the edge of the front porch, Suii went down to his belly and rolled to his back again. I notified dispatch to call CPS and get them over here STAT. A minute later, Suii's big tongue had the kids giggling as he bathed the tears from their faces and accepted additional belly scratches. There were a lot of questions I should have asked about my dog. He was behaving gently around these kids. He continued keeping them occupied as they wheeled out mom. A few minutes later, dad was walked out in handcuffs with a bandage over his arm.

"I'll own this entire city if that dog hurts my kids," Daryl said as he walked by. Neither of the children looked at him. It was sad that this occurred so often they were practically immune. Silently, I swore this would be the last time. If Melody wouldn't leave her husband, I planned to fight tooth and nail to get the kids removed.

Chapter Five

Suii whined for ten minutes after the children left with CPS. I placed my hand down at his head and he licked my fingers. Two more officers arrived as I began taking pictures. I rarely showed up first to a scene and if I'd wanted to, I could hand off the incident report to Officer Franks and I could then handle the supplemental. But I was determined to have the kids removed from the home if their mother didn't make the right decision, so I wanted lead on this case.

"That's a good K9 you got there," Franks said.

I'd just finished up with my pictures, Suii following closely by my side. "Yes, he is," I said with pride in my voice. The officers began chatting with me and, shock of shocks, I explained why I wanted the case. This was something I never did.

They didn't try to touch Suii, but their attitude was…accepting.

"He's got a drug cert too, doesn't he?" Franks asked.

"Yes, he's dual trained."

"Would a call in the middle of the night bother you?" Franks went on quickly before I could answer. "The drug task force works I-40 on weekends and inevitably we need a dog when there isn't one available."

Ah heck. It wouldn't kill me, though. "If you can limit it to two or three times a month I won't complain."

His smile was almost comical. I was known for complaining about everything.

I left the scene with my pictures, and three hours later, I had my finished report in hand. It included the accompanying paperwork with a use of K9 force document. Most people had no idea the amount of paperwork required to complete a police report. Added to this, I had Suii's record book to fill out now. It showed a successful apprehension with minimal injury to my suspect.

Suii and I made our way to Sergeant Spence's office.

Lou was on the phone, so I took a seat at his desk knowing from years of experience that he would shut his door if the call was private. He snapped his fingers at Suii and I released the leash. Suii accepted the attention Sergeant Spence applied to the scruff of his neck like he deserved it.

"Call me back when you have an answer," Lou said before hanging up the phone and turning his full attention to me. "Two weeks without a complaint against you. I'm impressed."

He exaggerated. I averaged about one a month if you didn't count verbal grumbles from co-workers. "I think Suii will get the complaint that goes with this report. If you plan on piling the dog's complaints with mine, I'll file a grievance." I had no intention of smiling, but something about Lou giving attention to Suii lightened my mood.

"Did the devil's playground freeze over?" Lou's grin went as big as mine.

"It's possible. Suii's a great dog." Suii gave a small whine like he understood my compliment.

"All these years and no one noticed your only problem is a dislike of people."

"I liked Tony." It was the first time I initiated conversation about my old partner.

The significance wasn't lost on me. It was time to move on with my life.

"We all liked Tony and he made you tolerable to be around. Suii seems to have the same effect. I'm glad it's working out."

I wasn't yet ready to thank Lou for hooking me up with Suii. Instead, I handed over the report with the use of force document on top. Lou read it and flipped through the rest of the paperwork.

"Good job, Suii." He reached in his drawer and pulled out a box of dog biscuits. I fought another smile. If I wasn't careful, Sergeant Spence would have Suii's trust and I'd be on the outs again.

After Lou signed off on the report, I hand-delivered a copy to the district attorney's office. I wanted Daryl in jail until the kids were safe. My mood cheered up when the DA agreed. After my shift, Suii and I went to the park and worked on commands. I needed the work more than Suii. And, it felt good to have something to do other than go home to eat a microwave dinner and kick back in front of the television. Because of my exceptional dog, life was changing quickly.

The next morning, I woke up with Suii lying on the foot of my bed. "You know, if I ever get married, this won't work?"

Suii barked his approval.

"As long as we're clear," I responded.

I got up and made my way into the kitchen to start the coffee. Suii trailed beside me and patiently waited for his morning kibbles. I found myself looking forward to what the day would hold.

Each morning when I woke, I found Suii farther up the bed. A week later, his massive head rested on the pillow beside mine. Before getting up to fetch my coffee, I scratched his neck and belly. Who needed a husband anyway?

On the one-month anniversary of having Suii, we made a trip to Tony's grave. The sadness was still there, but more distant. I spoke to the green grass covering Tony's coffin and introduced him to Suii. Suii remained solemn while I spoke to Tony about the active cases I had. No replies from either of them gave Tony and Suii a lot in common. I felt better when we turned to leave. Though I would miss him always, I knew Tony was part of my past and I had a life to live. I gave a small tug to Suii's leash and then watched in stunned disbelief as my dog raised his hind leg and desecrated Tony's grave.

It took a few seconds before laughter got the better of me. I knew Tony was laughing too. Suii would most definitely win a peeing contest between the two. I laughed until I cried, but they were healing tears. It was time to move on.

"Come on, partner. We have a job to do."

Suii's nub of a tail wagged the entire walk back to the car.

Chapter Six

It wasn't until the end of our second month that I got around to calling Jack Mallory and asking more questions about Suii's history.

"I expected this call within two weeks of you leaving here, not two months." Jack's gruff voice had me smiling immediately.

"You think I'm giving him back, don't you?"

He chuckled and little goosebumps covered my arms. "No, but I figured you want more information about your K9."

Jack was a smart man. Suii was mine. "Life has been interesting. What can you tell me?"

Jack didn't beat around the bush. "Suii was with his handler for four years. Officer Bradly was a great guy and Suii an exemplary K9. He lived in Bradly's home with his wife and two children. After Bradly's death, Tina, his wife, tried to adopt Suii, but it's against the rules, which only allow an active K9 to be with a certified officer. So, Suii came here to the K9 center."

That explained Suii's love of kids. My heart broke for Tina and the children who lost their father and his K9. It broke for Suii too.

Jack continued, "Suii went into a heavy state of depression after Bradly died. Don't give me any crap either. Dogs suffer just like humans. Maybe worse. You can't explain to a dog why these things happen; one day their handler is there and the next he isn't." Jack hesitated a moment. "I take it the two of you are getting along?"

My smile came back. "Suii's one of the best partners I've ever had."

Jack gave a low, pleased laugh. "I knew he was the dog for you before you ever saw him. I took him home when the guy before you came to choose his dog."

My grin widened. "You knew, huh?"

"I always know."

That made me happier for some reason. "How did he get a name like Suii?" I'd been curious about this for a while too.

"You didn't read his paperwork?"

Well darn. "No, I didn't think to look. Does it answer the question?"

"Suii is short for Suicide. That dog will tear a person to shreds and its suicide to go up against him."

I looked at Suii, who was watching me attentively. I gave him a loving pat on his large head. Jack and I spoke a little longer—small talk, but it didn't bother me. I liked listening to Jack's voice. Too bad he lived so far away. He was a man who wouldn't have a problem with a dog hogging pillow space.

After we hung up, I started doing a little research. It paid off and two phone calls later, I'd scheduled an appointment for Saturday. Our appointment came two days later.

I owned a small single-bench seat, four-wheel-drive truck and used it for non-work-related driving. Suii liked to hang his head out the sliding back window as I drove. It was nice that his slobber had a place to fall and didn't hurt the upholstery.

Suii began whining as we drew closer to our destination. He was uncontrollable by the time I parked the truck, and then Suii pulled me to the front door of the house. The door opened before I could knock.

"Suii," two boys yelled simultaneously.

This was Suii's family. Their mother, Tina, joined them on the front steps and threw her arms around Suii too. She was crying and so was I. It took another few minutes for their welcome hugs and licks to subside. Tina invited me inside. We sat at the kitchen table while the boys took Suii out back and played ball. Suii knew the routine well.

"Thank you for bringing him." She handed me a tissue and we both wiped our eyes.

"You might not thank me when it's time to leave. I had no idea how hard this would be." I truly didn't and now I could only imagine dragging Suii out of here and listening to him cry all the way home. Tina's boys would be heartbroken all over again too.

"It would be easier if you agree to bring him back again." She smiled at me with her wet, hopeful eyes.

"You'll have trouble keeping us away."

We spent two hours talking about her husband, the boys, and Suii. Leaving was as hard as I imagined. I explained to Suii the entire drive home that I would bring him back. He finally quieted down and licked my hand before pushing his head out the window.

Suii understood.

Over the next few months, my solved-case ratio increased to what it was with Tony. The other detectives were requesting K9s of their own. They made friends with Suii, and I was back in the fold. Beth's wedding loomed closer, and I finally returned the RSVP card with a plus one added. I could do this. Tony would have wanted Beth to be happy. I wanted it too.

I stepped out of my truck wearing a cream blouse and brown flowing pants. I'd asked for assistance from a boutique clerk close to my house because I was not up on wedding attendance fashion. I found a white bow tie at a thrift store and attached it to a piece of black elastic. Nope, it wasn't for me, it was for Suii. He was my plus one.

Beth and her new husband didn't mind that Suii came with me, and Suii remained on his best behavior while we watched the ceremony. Life went on and so did love. I reached over and gave Suii a gentle ruffle at his throat. He looked at me before turning his attention back to what was taking place in front of us. He understood that weddings were important.

Chapter Seven

After the New Year, we had a string of burglaries that were driving us crazy. Businesses were being hit downtown. It happened about once a week on random nights. No rhyme or reason that we could figure out. Patrols in the area were increased, but it did no good.

We knew we had two subjects because there were two different shoe prints. They took cash only and it surprised me how much money business owners left behind each day. Everything from soda money collected from employees to hundreds of dollars stored in office cabinets and drawers. The bad guys were quick and smart.

The city council complained to the chief of police and the chief breathed down Sergeant Spence's neck. No one was happy. The detective units began working stakeout. This was not my favorite job. Boredom was expected. We took four-hour shifts and still worked our day shifts.

Suii listened to me complain during our four hours. It was Saturday night and our boys, or girls with really large feet, were getting smarter. They'd hit the night before between four and five in the morning. We didn't have the manpower to cover the entire downtown area. It was also harder because we knew they were on foot. Several times we'd followed their tracks quite a distance away and never in the same direction. There were no vehicle lights to guide us. It sucked.

"Next weekend I'll take you to see Tina and the boys," I promised Suii. We went every two weeks and it had gotten easier to leave each time.

Suii gave a near silent bark knowing he needed to keep quiet and also knowing exactly what I said. I'd stopped speculating on what Suii understood and what he didn't. The dog knew every word I spoke and that was fact.

His low rumbling growl surprised me. My heartbeat accelerated as I peered into the dark and waited. I lowered my window an inch and a few minutes later heard glass breaking.

They'd hit last night and for some reason thought they'd be safe tonight.

I decided to check things out before calling dispatch. If a patrol officer was in the vicinity, it might tip off our guys before we could stop them from getting away. I quietly opened my door, stepped out, and opened Suii's. My vehicle's inside lights were disconnected so I wouldn't give away our presence. Suii didn't act excited or let out his usual whines. He was all business.

I held my gun in my right hand and a small flashlight, which I hadn't turned on yet, in the left with Suii's leash. Suii's hearing was better than mine. "Voran!" *Take the lead*! I whispered. He did exactly that. We rounded the front corner of the saddle and leather shop that had a small alley on the far side. I heard crunching glass and Suii let out another low growl. I quickly followed Suii around the corner into the alley. A man was clearing the window with another standing and waiting for him.

Crap, I should have informed dispatch. I brought up my gun. "Stop right there. Police," I shouted. With my command, Suii's growls were no longer soft. The guys froze.

Keeping a tight hold on Suii's lead, I pressed the flashlight with my thumb. It would only stay on as long as I pressed down. To get it to remain lit you had to twist the bottom. It wasn't happening, because Suii was pulling on the lead.

"Bleib!" *Hold*, I told him. He stopped straining, but never stopped growling.

"Put your hands where I can see them." I took a few steps closer when both men lifted their arms. The guy I saw climb out of the building fidgeted and I knew he planned to take off. He turned and started running. "Fass," *Attack*, I yelled as I released Suii's leash.

I trained my gun on the other guy and let Suii do his thing. Growls and screaming man-sounds came within seconds. Now, the other guy acted antsy. He lowered his hands.

"Hands up," I yelled as I clicked on the mic to my radio.

"Backup in the alley next to the saddle shop," I said. I was the only female on duty and everyone knew I was on stakeout. Leaving off my badge number was completely outside dispatch protocol, but I needed my focus in front of me.

"Get him off, get him off," the guy Suii held screamed and begged.

My guy turned completely so his back was to me and lowered his hands. I thought he would run, and there was no way I was shooting him in the back. I holstered my gun to grab my Taser as everything went into slow motion.

He turned and I saw the flash of a gun at the same time he fired. I dove to the ground transferring my Taser to my other hand and drawing my gun. My adrenaline was pumping too hard to know if I took a hit. It didn't matter; I could never return fire in time.

I heard the blast of another shot before my gun cleared my holster. At that instant, one hundred and fifty pounds of ticked off Rottweiler came to my rescue. Suii hit the guy high in the chest and I saw the gun fly several feet away. I quickly glanced toward the other man. He was rolling on the ground. I had no idea if he had a weapon. Training took over. Where there was one gun there were two.

"Don't move, don't move," I yelled as I turned my gun his way.

I took a quick glance back at Suii, who was still growling. The man beneath him was struggling, but Suii didn't get off him. Seconds later, two patrol cars pulled up, their lights flashing into the alley.

"Cover this guy; he might be armed," I yelled as I ran toward Suii. I kicked the guy's gun a few more feet away. "Suii. Aus." *Let go*, I said.

Suii rolled off the guy without getting up, which was the first indication I had that something was wrong. Two officers pulled the guy away after Suii's jaws relaxed and released him. I was already on my knees and immediately felt the sticky wetness of Suii's blood. His tongue lolled out as shallow pants escaped his throat.

"No, no, no," I cried over and over. "No, Suii, please." His big dark eyes looked into mine. He raised his paw and it came down so it rested on my arm. The air expelled from his chest and his eyes glazed over.

Suii was gone.

Chapter Eight

When a police K9 dies in the line of duty, the handler plans the funeral. I couldn't have done it if it weren't for the other detectives and officers. Suii's death put me in a place I hadn't been since Tony's passing. Tony battled cancer for a year and his death was unfortunately expected. His wife took center stage when it came to support from the department. That's as it should be. With Suii's death, I was center stage. I grumbled a little, complained a lot, but accepted the help. One of the female officers insisted on going home with me until the funeral. Completely over the top, and I knew Lou had something to do with it. Justine gave me no time alone and though I wouldn't admit it, I needed someone around.

The day of the funeral was cold and windy. The local newspaper wrote a huge article about

Suii, making it the biggest news in the county. Sergeant Spence told me they expected a packed house. The bagpipes got me every time and it was no different now. I heard them as I stepped from Lou's vehicle, my crisp dress uniform uncomfortable yet comforting. I wiped my eyes trying to prepare myself for what was to come. We were early, but so were the sorrowful sounds of "Going Home" blowing through the pipes.

Several officers waited inside. They hugged me tightly, showing their support. Lou steered me up front where a picture of me and Suii sat on a high table. I remembered the day someone took it. I was showing off Suii's abilities and half the department stood in the police parking area and watched.

Next to the picture, a wooden urn held Suii's ashes. I'd picked it out with Justine's help. There was a silver inscribed plate on top. My tears flowed over as I read it again.

*The heart and soul of a K9 lives forever.*
*His four paws enjoy the path of endless walks.*
*His food bowl is always full.*
*His fearless sacrifice never forgotten.*
*Rest in peace, Suii.*

My fingertips ran over the words. I'd missed him every second over the past five days. I needed him so badly. A hand rested on my back and I turned to see Tina standing beside me. Her boys were with her and all three of them cried. I dropped to my knees and gave the boys a tight hug. I was so glad they came even knowing how hard this must be. Their father had been dead for little more than a year.

"He saved my life," I whispered.

I pulled myself together for the boys' sake and managed to give Tina a long hug.

"Thank you for bringing him to see us so often," she said.

Suii needed it as much as Tina and the boys did. "I'm so glad you came." It was all I could say. My tears kept me from speaking further. I looked around and realized the auditorium was almost full. Several people stepped aside at the front double doors as handlers with their K9s entered one after the other. The sight was amazing.

Jack Mallory entered behind them. Our eyes met as I watched him walk closer. His strong arms circled around me and offered comfort. A few moments later, we took our seats in the front row as the service began. Officer Franks told the story of Suii successfully apprehending a suspect during a domestic. One after another, officers come forward and spoke about Suii's short time with us. I took a deep breath and allowed their words to settle over me.

With Jack on one side and Tina and her boys on the other, I cried for my friend and partner. Sergeant Spence spoke last. He told of Suii saving my life and giving his own so his handler could live. When he finished, he picked up Suii's urn. I stood and walked forward. Lou placed it in my arms. It was my choice to keep Suii's ashes. The box was now all that I had left of him. Slowly everyone made their way outside for the last call. We turned on our radios.

The dispatcher from the night of Suii's death spoke over the radio. I could hear her sobs between each word. "K9 Officer David Sixteen." She took a deep breath and continued. "K9 Officer David Sixteen last call." Pause. "K9 Officer David Sixteen out of service."

A hush surrounded me when our radios went silent.

It was over and I without a partner again.

So many people offered condolences. I woodenly shook their hands. The K9 handlers in attendance waited until the last person walked away. My heart broke further at the sight of their dogs by their sides. Jack guided me over and we walked down the line shaking hands.

"Can I drive you home?" Jack asked when we were done.

"Sounds good. Let me tell my sergeant." I walked a few feet away and spoke to Lou.

"I expect you at work tomorrow," he said as he pulled me close for a quick hug. My sergeant knew me well.

I returned to Jack and we walked to his car. He looked good wearing his state police dress uniform. I guess I knew he was certified, but it just hadn't registered. What a job it must be to work with K9s and their handlers every day.

"How are you doing?" He asked after pulling out of the parking lot.

I couldn't help running my fingers back and forth across the top of Suii's urn. "I'll be okay... someday."

"You're a great handler. When that day comes, you call me and we'll find you another dog."

The words hurt. "I don't think so."

"I know so, but we won't worry about it now."

Other than giving him directions to my house, we didn't speak much after that. "Do you want to come in?" I asked after he pulled up in front of my townhouse.

"No, I need to head back to Tucson. Will you be okay alone?"

From the corner of my eye, I saw Mr. Knock-toes holding Craptzu. He just stood there and it occurred to me that he was waiting for me to get out of the car. I turned to Jack. "I'll survive. Thank you for the ride."

I waved Jack away before turning to my neighbor.

"I read about you and your dog in the paper. I'm very sorry."

"Thank you, I appreciate it."

Little Crap whined a bit and I couldn't help reaching my hand out and scratching beneath his chin. "Would you like to come inside for some tea?"

He gave me a long look. "I'd love to. Do you have anything stronger to add to the tea?"

I smiled. Boy did I.

Chapter Nine

The first few months were the hardest. This time, my fellow officers weren't letting me get away with the standoff routine. I wasn't quite sure if it was them or if Suii had softened me. But whatever it was, it worked. The walls I'd constructed years ago were gone. Even so, I refused to be partnered up with anyone again. Lou surprisingly gave in with little more than a shake of his head.

I quickly got back into the thick of things. While driving, I talked over my cases with both Tony and Suii. Don't worry, they still weren't answering. Speaking out loud helped me connect the dots.

A little over six months after Suii's death, my cell phone rang toward the end of my shift.

"Detective Jolett speaking."

"It's Jack."

My heart skipped a beat. It felt so good to hear his voice. "Hi," I said a little breathlessly. I probably sounded like an idiot.

"I spoke to your sergeant and he wants you driving here first thing in the morning to look at a dog."

Crap, I was so not ready. "I can't, Jack."

"You don't have a choice. I just want you to have a look. No pressure."

No pressure my butt. "It's a waste of time. I'm not taking on a new K9."

"I'll expect you here at ten." He ended the call.

I left my house at seven the next morning. My emotions jumped between sad and angry. I was the bad-luck partner and I didn't need someone else dying on me. I was in a complete snit by the time I walked into the kennel.

"I worried you'd disobey a direct order," Jack said as he rose from changing out a water dish in one of the kennels.

"The last thing I need is my pay docked. So I'm here; show me the darned dog."

Jack smiled and I fought back a small thrill. Darn he was nice looking.

"Come meet Mika." Jack walked over a few cages and opened the door. Mika was a German Shepherd and didn't look like anything special. "He's new, but a darn fine K9."

Why did my heart drop? I swore to myself that I didn't want another dog but it was really a lie. Seeing Mika, I knew he wasn't the one for me. There was no connection. I gave Mika a small scratch and moved away from the pen. I had a long drive back home and there was no way I was staying one minute longer than I had to.

I turned slightly and noticed a black ball of fur in the back of the next cage.

"Don't even look. Her disposition is horrible."

"It's a lab. Just how bad can she be?" I asked in exasperation.

"You'll be sorry." Jack closed Mika's cage and opened the other.

Dark brown eyes gazed into mine as the dog unfolded herself and slowly walked over. I went to my knees. She buried her big dark head against my chest as I scratched behind her ears. "What's her name?"

"Bell."

"Short for?"

"Belladonna as in the poison," Jack grumbled.

"This is the dog you wanted me to see, isn't it?"

This time, Jack smiled full out and my heart skipped a beat. "She's your dog; I knew it from the moment she came in. Did you pack a bag for two weeks of training?"

My certification for the first six-weeks of training was good for three years. I was only required to attend two weeks with a new dog. "Yes." And I really hated to admit I packed for the entire two weeks just in case.

"Good, we'll get started right now. Bell can be a little lazy and she needs a strong hand."

I looked into Bell's eyes. "My kind of dog."

A note from the author:

I sent this story to my editor on November 1, 2014. Sadly, at that time, twenty Police K9's died in the line of duty in 2014. I was lucky enough to work with one of these incredible dogs for a year. He belonged to my partner Jim. Those memories will forever be the most exciting and rewarding time I spent in law enforcement. Astro is retired now and lives with Jim, his wife, and their two boys. I never thought a K9 could be so child friendly until I saw Astro with children. Thank you to all the special K9's and their handlers. Be safe!

This story originally release in "10-Code: Written By Cops Honoring The Ultimate Sacrifice." Police Chief Scott Silverii came up with the idea for a group of police officer/writers to write stories, dedicate each of theirs to a fallen officer they knew personally, and donate all proceeds to the National Law Enforcement Officers Memorial Fund. Thank you Scott for including me.

*This edition of The Forever Team is also for my grandchildren—Nathan, Caden, Eric, Davin, Benjamin, Jaedyn, Ashlyn, Shaylee, Brycen, and Liam; I love you. Suii is the dog I hope you have in your life. If not, come to grandma's house and play with Dizzy. She loves you as much as I do.*

About the Author

Retired Police Detective Suzie Ivy spends her time writing, relaxing, and playing with her dog, Dizzy, a Rottweiler with anxiety issues. Suzie is a contributing writer for UniformStories.com and now and then pens something new on her blog badluckdetective.com. She is a USA Today Best-Selling Author of the book "Play" written under one of her three pen names. You can find more about her paranormal and steamy romance books at www.wickedstorytelling.com.

Made in the USA
Las Vegas, NV
15 May 2022